UNEASY BEGINNINGS

Uneasy Beginnings

by

Simon Kurt Unsworth &
Benjamin Kurt Unsworth

Black Shuck Books
www.BlackShuckBooks.co.uk

First published in the UK by Black Shuck Books, 2020

978-1-913038-50-2

To Steve and Andrew, best friends both.
Simon Kurt Unsworth

To Sam, who keeps me insane.
Benjamin Kurt Unsworth

Introduction

This book is, of course, an act of grandest nepotism and I make no apologies for that. This is a book by me and my boy, and I think that's fucking great. I would hope, though, that it is not without merit as a story collection and it can be enjoyed as that. It is, also, a kind of experiment. How can a collection of short stories be an experiment, you may ask? Well, if you have a minute, indulge me. Sit down, if you aren't sat already, get a drink to hand, get comfortable. Turn the world down and let me explain.

A while ago, my son Ben began to write. I mean, not just write but *write*, seemingly every waking moment he was with me. I'd wonder where my aged, battered Mac was and invariably find it with him, perched on his knee as he hammered out stories, scripts for Doctor Who audios and TV dramas, jotted ideas down and generally writing up a storm. Sometimes (despite my sagest recommendations) he'd start one thing before finishing the previous, he always seemed to have several files open at once, he'd write instead of reading, he'd write whilst watching television, in the morning and late at night and at all points in between. On occasion I'd wrest my Mac back off him and find internet pages open at bizarre subjects he'd been researching which is, as far as I can tell, par for the course for anyone living with a writer and using their computers.

On rainy evening, while we walked the dogs, Ben'd tell me about the things he was writing and less often, he'd ask advice and I'd try to guide and encourage him as best I could. As a father it made me proud to see him being so creative, as a writer I was a little jealous of the sheer scale of his creativity and the energy he brought to the keyboard and as a man going grey with age I marvelled at his youth and optimism. He wasn't so much grappling with his muse as he was wrestling it to the ground and demanding its attention, demanding it listen to him and to no one else. It was (and still is, because at the time of writing he's still doing it) a little awe-inspiring.

The question was, was what Ben was writing any good? In that ever-increasing mass of words, was there quality?

I don't know. In those first months I didn't read any of them because if I read hadn't read them they could be masterpieces, and the worst thing in the world would have been to discover that they weren't, that they were just good, or merely mediocre, or disappointingly rubbish. Actually, no, that would have been the second worst thing; the first worst thing would have been to have to tell Ben that I thought they were just good, or merely mediocre, or disappointingly rubbish. So I made excuses and told Ben to keep writing and that I'd read them one day but not just then. And Ben, all credit to him, carried on writing and I carried on critiquing the ideas he floated with me on those late night dog walks, sometimes pointing him in the direction of stories similar to what he was doing or towards works that might give him insights into how good fiction could work, sometimes just being positive and hoping and enjoying his passion.

It did make me think, though. Every writer I know (and I know a few – it's one of the real benefits of this published life) has old stories written on scraps of paper and saved on floppy discs and scrawled in notebooks and hanging around on old laptops, things written before they'd found their voice or even, often, their talent, things they like but they don't necessarily like enough, things they're often deeply proud of whilst recognising their (often immense) flaws. I know I have things I wrote when I was twelve or thirteen and nothing could make me part with them even if I'm not sure I'd ever actually want to show them to anyone. But...but...that's not quite true. I've always wanted to write something into which I could incorporate them, to have my cake and eat it: read this new piece and while you do you can look upon my early works, ye readers, and agree that whilst they aren't great they fit this other concept I've come up with quite brilliantly! And more seriously, I figured, there's a universe of finished and half-finished things lurking out beyond the peripheries and anyone with with access to them could, if they were so inclined, read them and see how a writer moved from, say, ripping off Stephen King to finding a way of telling stories that was unique, that was their signature style. And, if we're dreaming, you could find someone who was at that early stage of writing *now*, you could include their work and maybe in the future years there'd be more adult, more complete things of theirs to read and compare these early efforts to and maybe, just maybe, there'd would be something to learn about writing from those comparisons.

See what I've done there?

Because the thing is, I'm just about arrogant enough to believe that maybe people might want to read my early stuff and that it's good enough to read, and I've always been just about confident enough to think that any son of mine was clearly going to be a chip off the old block and a natural wordsmith, dreamweaver and imagineer to his very core, and that people would be interested in his stuff too. The cakes of both worlds, storytelling and literary experiment, were calling, but first there was a thing I had to do and it was pretty damn terrifying.

I had to read Ben's stuff.

So I girded my loins and I did, and you know what? The stories turned out to be pretty good, if clearly the writing of a person who'd not actually experienced much in the world and who was still learning. There were ideas there that, even to my entirely biased eyes, that seemed pretty good and some evidence of wit and talent and imagination. Steve Shaw, blessed guru of the publishing world and a man of great taste and refinement, had said he'd consider publishing the collection as part of the Shadows series, so I made Ben a deal: I wouldn't rewrite or change his stuff but I would approach his stories as the best editor I could be, and for his part he'd need to be ready to hear criticism and to make what changes he thought would improve things based on what he heard. Between us we'd produce a short collection that would serve as a look back at my career and as a pin for the front of his possible career. Along the way I hoped we'd have fun and maybe make something we could show to people and be proud of.

So Ben picked the stories of his he thought were the most complete (and trust me, we had long conversations about what being 'complete' meant for a story at the first draft stage), sent them to me and started I to edit them.

It's not been an easy ride. We've argued, although thankfully not too badly, and had to come to compromise positions. I've had to remember that Ben is only young and that his skin maybe isn't as thick as mine, and Ben's had to learn to accept the simple fact that a human body, no matter how hard it's thrown, will always come off worse if it collides with a stone pillar and he shouldn't argue with his senior editor about that. We've been back and forth, over some bumps on the way that have slowed us down but they've never quite beaten us. We've done things like spend several hours in a café in Greece discussing plot points in one story only to end up not using it, and on another dealt with the infuriating fact that Ben insisting remembering that I'd once said to him it was okay to disagree with your editors because sometimes the author knows the feeling of the story better than the editor ever will. Nightmare stuff but still, we got there in the end.

So that's what this is, this book you're currently holding (or, I suppose, e-reader document you're perusing). It's a collection of maybe rough, possibly raw and perhaps only just halfway-polished stories, yes, but hopefully they're ones you can enjoy on their own basic terms. It's also a chance to see where a writer comes from and where another might start. Can you see the progression of my work between these stories and my later work? I don't know but I'd hope so. If Ben writes more will we see the same kind of progressions? Again, I don't know but I'd hope so. As long as he enjoys the writing he does, I'll be happy in his enjoyment, and if he doesn't take his writing any further then I'll at least know we did this together and that feels pretty special if I'm honest.

Oh, and a note: there are four of my stories and three of Ben's in this collection. I'm not telling which is which. Want to know who wrote what? Read them and then, if you can, guess.

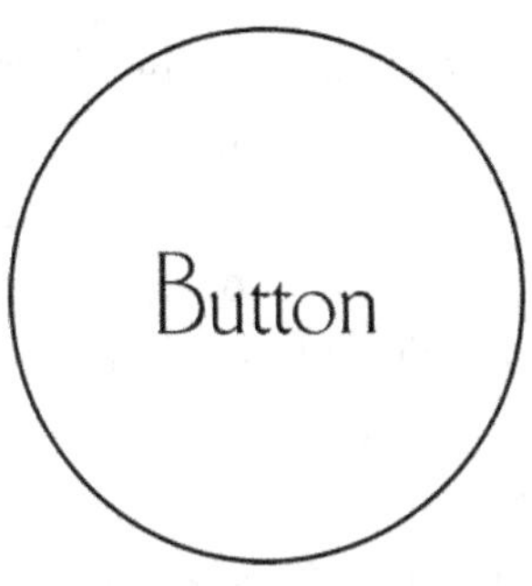

Button

When something fell past Bruno as he walked along the hallway, his reaction was as instinctive as it was quick. Twisting, he thrust his left hand out, palm up, and caught the object. Surprised, he looked at his hand, which had automatically made a fist about the falling something. Ordinarily he was clumsy and uncoordinated and unable to catch even large, slow-moving things and so this tiny moment felt like a victory, although over what he was not sure. Himself, perhaps.

Keeping his fist clenched tight, Bruno tried to work out what the object was; it felt small and round, like a coin, but it did not have the cold detachment that he usually experienced when touching metal. It was warm against his skin, like sun-heated plastic. *Odd*, he thought, looking up the stairway at his landing where the object must have come from. In the shadowed emptiness, the pale streak of the banister glowed. Nothing else moved. Sighing, feeling his moment of triumph slip away, he opened his hand.

It was a button.

The button was old and scuffed and made of wood. There were four small holes set about its centre and its edge was worn and, in one place, chipped. It was lying nestled at the base of the ball of his thumb, caught in the soft valley formed there between thumb and palm. The wooden surface was mottled yet shining, the smooth patina of age worn into it like a varnish. Grinning, Bruno thought *I caught a button!* and then tried to curl his fingers and pinch it between his fingertips.

It would not move.

Laughing at his own clumsiness, so soon returned, Bruno gave up trying to catch the button with the fingers from the left hand and instead used his right. It still would not move. Tugging at it did nothing other than send a curious shooting pain along his thumb and out across his palm. Growing irritated, Bruno shook his hand furiously, hoping to dislodge the button, but it remained stubbornly attached to his skin. He pulled at it again, getting his fingernails as far under its edge as he could, and this time the pain as he pulled made him cry out in surprise. It was like biting into tinfoil – a nervy, bloodless jolt that was over as quickly as it had begun.

Annoyed now, Bruno shook his hand again, flailing it back and forth with growing anger. *Someone must be playing a joke on me,* he thought, *one that's not very funny. They've coated the button with glue and now it's stuck to me and when I find out who it is, they'll be sorry.* Only, even as he thought it, Bruno was unconvinced. He didn't have many friends, and certainly none who would go to the kind of trouble that this situation indicated. And if it wasn't a friend, then who was it? And why had they done this to him?

Bruno took to trying to pry the button from his skin with a knife as his normal bedtime slipped quietly past him. Taking the sharpest implement he possessed, he worked it under the edge of the button, wiggling it gently back and forth and using the motion to slip the blade further and further under. There came a point, however, past which the knife would not go; it came up against something hard, presumably where the adhesive had bonded most strongly with his skin, and where pressing was the most painful. It was like probing an open ulcer with his tongue, he thought. Painful, yet curiously addictive. Eventually, he forced himself to put the knife down. *I'm sat at my kitchen table with a button stuck to me*, he thought, his anger fading and becoming embarrassment.

Bruno's sleep was not easy that night, and he woke early the next day. His waking thought was that he had had a terribly bad dream whose insanity was only matched by the growing feeling of frustration he felt whilst within it, but his hopes dwindled when he found the button still attached to his hand. He got up, dressed, went to his kitchen and made himself a coffee, deliberately ignoring the offending item until he was sat at his table and as calm as he could be. Then, he risked looking.

He found when he pushed at it that the button was still stuck firmly to him. He must have also cut himself with the knife yesterday and not realised it, as there was now a thin red line stretching out perhaps a quarter of an inch on either side of the button. Running his finger over the line, it felt warm and tingled at his touch. Groaning, Bruno placed his head flat on the table. It looked like he'd managed to give himself blood poisoning as well! How much worse could this get?

The rest of the morning passed in a long blur of pulling and prodding and sharp pain, but the button remained as immovable as it had been the day before. What was in some ways worse was that Bruno needed to leave the house. He needed milk and bread and other essential items, and it was bright summer outside. How could he wear gloves? People would see, just as they would see the button if he went about with his hands naked. He tried placing a sticking plaster over the button, but it felt horrible and painful. He tried covering the button with a bandage, but again the pressure of the cloth on the button sent that odd, sharp pain coursing through him. He noted as well that the pain was travelling slightly further up his arm each time that he experienced it; where last night it had been confined to his hand, and this morning it had definitely only been getting to his wrist, now it was reaching almost to his elbow.

By mid-afternoon, the red lines were a deeper and darker red, although they did not seem to have grown in length too much. Now when he touched them, he could clearly feel that they were hot. Perhaps the blood poisoning was from whatever adhesive had been used, and not from his own prodding with the knife? The skin around the button was also beginning to feel strange; when he pressed on it, it seemed to slip against the flesh underneath ever so slightly, as though its connection to muscles and tendons was becoming weaker. Bruno was getting worried, although he had thought of a plan. He would not leave the house yet; he could do without most things for a while. No, he was going to have a bath.

When he was younger, Bruno had accidentally glued two of his fingers, both to each other and to his personal stereo, with superglue. Although (with the loss of a patch of skin) he had freed them from the stereo, the fingers themselves had proved impossible to separate. Eventually, Bruno's mother had ordered him into the bath, where she claimed the mixture of heat, water and chemicals produced by his skin as he sweated would loosen the glue sufficiently enough to allow his digits to be freed. Sure enough, after an hour in the bath followed by some careful picking with a knife, his fingers had been detached from one another. *I can't believe I didn't think of this earlier*, he thought as he sank with a sigh into the hot water, *this'll work*.

It didn't.

Tenacious as a limpet, the button stayed attached to his skin. When Bruno looked closely, he could even see what looked like threads passing between the small holes at the centre of the button, pink lines laid almost flush to the button's surface. The red marks on his skin had grown deeper, and the skin itself seemed to be splitting at the centre of them, close to the button. Bruno squeezed his arm at the wrist and was alarmed to find that the disconnected, slithering sensation had grown further as well, as though encouraged by the heat of the bath. Now it stretched, he found, up to his mid-forearm. Scared, angry and confused in equal measure, he dressed and went downstairs. He had vodka, he remembered. It might not help with the button, but it would certainly help take his mind off things.

~

Bruno's clumsiness meant he had never really been interested in DIY, but over the years he had managed to collect a stockpile of basic tools. Screwdrivers, used more often than not to stir paint, lay in his kitchen drawers, as did a hammer, some nails and a hacksaw. The hacksaw's blade was rusted almost through and snapped when he pressed it, which left only the axe. Where he had got the ugly thing he had no idea, but its chopping edge was still keen despite the pitting of rust across its head. It was a heavy object, but he found he could lift it with one hand, which was good. Tears in his eyes, he raised it as high as he could, his right arm at full extension above him. His left was stretched out along the edge of the kitchen table, a tie knotted tightly above the bicep. In the moment before he allowed gravity to take hold, he wondered miserably how he had come to this place.

In the last twenty-four hours, things had gotten worse; his skin moved easily now when he touched it, sloughing and skiing across the surface of the flesh underneath. It was like wearing a warm, pink coat rather than skin. The button, as firmly attached as ever, now had thick pink threads crossing and re-crossing its centre, going from hole to tiny hole. His skin had split completely along the red lines, curling under the slits' edges, making a smooth, round-edged hole about an inch across with the button at its centre. It looked for all the world as though the button was now sitting on top of a buttonhole. When he tugged at the button, the pain was accompanied by a feeling of something pulling deep inside his arm. It was horrifying, and even more embarrassing. His arm looked stupid, made more so by the raised red bumps that had risen in a neat line up the inside of his wrist to the elbow. When he prodded the lumps, they moved ever so slightly under the skin, and increased pressure on them gave the lumps a distinct shape. Buttons. *Lumps like buttons?* he asked himself, but that only started the tears again; he had to stop thinking like that.

In the slowest part of the early morning, Bruno had made his mind up that he was going to hospital, and had got as far as the front door before he stopped. He couldn't. He *couldn't*. All his life, people had laughed at him; too tall in his first years at school, too fat in his later ones, he stood out. Too amiable and laid back to be good at presenting himself well, too relaxed to care about his appearance, his life had been a mess of half-formed friendships, of jeering peers and being looked down upon. And this? It would be discovered, and only give them something else to laugh at, something else to mark against him and condescend to him about. Going to the hospital would mean going out in public, exposing himself to embarrassment, laughter, cruelty. Weeping vodka-scented tears and clutching his front door frame, Bruno had fallen to his knees before pushing the door shut and crawling back inside his home.

Earlier, he had tried one last rational thing; he had sorted through every shirt, pair of pants, bag and coat that he owned to see if any of them had the same sort of buttons as was now stuck so steadfastly to his hand. None did.

So, the axe.

With the help of the numbing swathe of vodka (his drink of choice now), Bruno had come to a decision. It was a simple solution, although drastic. Cut the arm off, and things would be better. Cut the arm off and the button would be gone. No more embarrassment, no more pain, no more slipsliding skin. First, he practiced raising and lowering the axe, slowly placing it just above his elbow. He pressed, making a red line appear on his skin. *An aiming point*, he thought, *like a pencil line drawn on wood. I'll have to hit hard. I need to get through the bone and get the arm off entirely and then ring the ambulance before I pass out.* He raised the axe, feeling its weight in his hand.

His arms shivered. His teeth clenched. The axe fell.

There was a deep *chunk* as the axe blade bit deep. Bruno screamed out loud, a hoarse wail of anguish. He had moved his left arm at the last minute and the axe had done damage only to the wooden surface of his table. *Coward!* he cried out again, a hopeless call of misery, and loosened the tie around his bicep. The blood rushed back into his arm, and the neat lumps throbbed happily. Weeping, Bruno looked at his hand once more. He had a button stuck to him, a button sitting on top of a buttonhole.

A buttonhole.

Made to be unbuttoned. Perhaps if he did that, the button might fall off, go? Desperate and hopeful, Bruno did the only thing he could think of.

He undid the button.

A Lust for Ghosts

Fred Darvill loved ghosts.

He wasn't afraid of spending the night in a haunted house or camping in damp mausoleums because they were his thing, ever since 1992. He'd watched a fake-news broadcast about ghosts and been hooked from there. Fred didn't believe ghosts were necessarily evil or tragic, just the dead locked in a series of events, repeating a major tragedy or clinging to a certain place.

About a month ago, BAG (British Association of Ghostwatchers, a group he was a keen member of) had invited him to Castlespire Manor in the north of Cumbria. They had called him and asked if they would check out the ghost and give an opinion on the validity of the supernatural claim. BAG were also allowed to confirm or deny a claim of ghosts and whether they should be put on the national charter of approved haunted houses.

~

The aged Volvo rolled up the drive towards an imposing house captured in the sun's gaze. Castlespire Manor could be seen from the nearest homes, two miles away. It loomed over its surroundings, and Fred was a bit apprehensive about the visit because, actually, so was BAG. The owners, Maeve and Joseph Frostfall, had filed two claims in the past, both of which had been denied, and BAG now wanted to shut the pair up and stop them being a nuisance to the organisation. Just humour them and leave. Everyone in BAG and the surrounding villages knew they were just doing it for the money and the tourists.

After enduring the twisting roads and poor weather on his journey, Fred finally came to a halt. A thick mist was descending off the three surrounding hills and would be on them soon. The clouds were almost black and a devilish downpour seemed imminent. Fred got out the car but had misjudged the amount of space available. Thumping loudly, the door banged into a stone wall, denting it underneath the handle. The cigarette that Fred had been rolling dropped into the wet grass as he assessed the damage. Not too nasty, but bad enough considering the miniscule wage he had and the outstanding MOT payment that was still due.

As he was doing his assessment of his old car, he hadn't noticed a man dressed in your typical farmer outfit and a woman in a cream dress adorned with black roses walk up to the vehicle. Her dress seemed out of place, considering the weather.

"Good day. You are Mr Darvill?" spoke the woman. Though looking old she spoke with youthful vigour.

"Right. Yup. That's me. I assume you're the Frostfalls?" He shook Joseph's hand, which was old and crusty, then Maeve's, which wasn't crusty but was sweaty. He turned around, pulled a large suitcase and rucksack from the car and shut the door, accepting the dent yet cursing wildly in his head.

The three chatted for a while as they walked over frosty grass towards the large manor. All the windows were tinted red and creepers, vines and an assortment of invasive plants had practically covered the house. It definitely fitted the stereotypical haunted house. But even then, *stereotype?* Surrounding the house was a layer of tall trees, short on greenery but covered in crisp brown and yellow leaves that were conspicuously chattering in the background. The stream in the nearest field sounded more like vicious waves crashing into the sharp rocks on a desolate beach. This place did have it's *peculiarities*.

Once inside the great manor, Darvill put his bag down in the vestibule and continued through to a large area with a dining hall to the left, a staircase directly in front of him, another room to the right and a doorway (presumably leading to the kitchen) to the right of that. Spiders had been having a party, covering most surfaces in a thin layer of cobwebs.

"How long are you planning on staying?" asked Joseph. Fred was pretty sure he detected a twang of Scottish in his voice. Possibly he was a quarter or half Scottish. His wife however was pure, posh English.

"Probably tonight and tomorrow, but longer if necessary. I think there's an inn in Little

Hodbury so I'm probably staying there tonight." replied Fred

"There's no need for that, Mr Darvill. We've assembled a makeshift bed for you in the dining hall." Maeve said.

"Really? Well, ok. Will you be staying over as well?"

"Grief no." Joseph cut in. "Me and my wife will be in our cottage just along the farm track. However we'll check on you at 8am."

"So about this ghost?"

"Ghosts. Plural. Only appear after dusk. Probably be out in the next hour. Do you need us to stick around?"

"No. It'd be better if I was alone." He turned around a collected his bags. Both of the Frostfalls stood in the hall, holding hands and staring at Fred. He shambled into the dining hall and put his suitcases onto the rotting table, which groaned in protest. Cobwebs flew everywhere, including some into the BAG member's face. Making an echoing click, Fred unlatched the suitcase and proceeded to remove six cameras, audio equipment, sets of cabling and power supplies, and place them on the table. He hadn't bothered to include anything else. This was to be a very superficial investigation.

"Well, Joseph and I will be off." Maeve gripped his hand tightly in hers. "If you want the most haunted rooms in the house, check the kitchen and the upstairs landing. A woman named Melanie Stokes committed suicide in the kitchen thirty years ago and a young child named Alex Berry was hung by his father on the landing." With that unnerving statement, Maeve released his hand then followed her husband out of the house and along the track, age not slowing her. Outside, the mist had dropped from the hills and closed in, swallowing Castlespire Manor.

For the next half hour, Fred set up cameras in the sitting room, downstairs hall, upstairs landing, the child's nursery/bedroom and the master bedroom, and the oscilloscope in the dining hall. After this the man went to set up the final camera in the kitchen, he found a can of beans and sausages, bowl and spoon. They must have been left by Joseph or Maeve. He had a hankering for a pie of some sorts, his usual Tuesday supper, but he would have to make do. Fred pried opened one of the cans of beans, scooped out the contents, plopped it into the porcelain bowl then carried it into the dining room. He'd eat it cold. He glanced at the watch on his right wrist – 19:05 – time to settle down and begin the "surveillance".

~

The next morning, Joseph and Maeve arrived and knocked on the front door at exactly 8am. Fred came to the door with all his belongings and let the pair of owners in.

"So? What's the verdict about Castlespire?" Joseph asked, "It got to be haunted. Must be!"

"I'm sorry. There were a few ruffles but I really don't think this is a haunted house. Old maybe, but not haunted." Fred attempted to move past the pair but Joseph cut in front of him and ran halfway up the creaky staircase.

"Naw. It has to be haunted. Trust me!" Joseph's voice raised slightly.

"Listen Mr Frostfall, I know you think the house is haunted but I strongly suspect it isn't, and that's what I'll be telling BAG," replied Fred.

"Come with me, Mr Darvill!" he hollered down the stairs. Fred slowly trailed after him up the staircase after leaning the suitcase and bag against the banisters. The male Frostfall was at the top on the landing now, whilst his wife stood, arms crossed, in the hall by a set of drawers.

"I stood there two years ago and all my hairs stood on end! Multiple times have I stood by that beam and felt an eerie presence watching me, and Maeve once saw an apparition of a noose under that beam also! THIS HOUSE IS HAUNTED!" hollered Joseph. Spittle formed in the corners of his mouth and was flying everywhere, whilst his face was turning the colour of a sun dried tomato.

"No, Joseph Frostfall. It. Is. Not. Now I must be on my way." The man turned around to go back down to the main hall and vestibule when suddenly a sharp pain pierced his shoulder. Fred's balance was lost and he stumbled to his knees. His left hand sprang out to catch the wooden banister but instead of it providing support, he tumbled through the rotting oak, crashing onto the landing floor below. In his shoulder was a small sharp wooden stake. It stung and he could feel dribbles of blood soaking his back.

He lay on the floor and stared up at the

blurred figure. An attempt to lift himself failed miserably, and splinters dug deeper in his hand and arm.

"Well Mr Darvill. Even though you wield little faith you may still help us in our plight."

To his left the woman, wearing the same cream and black rose dress as yesterday, shuffled towards him, slipped her fragile arms underneath his and began to yank him towards the central staircase with strength Fred thought no OAP could possess. It was about this time that his eyelids fluttered and closed, as he fell unconscious.

~

Later, straining, Fred opened his eyes. He was back on the upstairs landing, though his feet were not on anything solid. His wrists were in pain and were clamped in steel cuffs attached to the ceiling, and his feet were clamped to the wall with slightly looser cuffs. The stake had been removed from his shoulder and heavy padding and bandages had been applied. As the glaze over his eyes cleared, he could finally make out Mrs Frostfall, standing with her arms crossed next to the banister which he crashed through earlier that day. Night was setting in and an orange glare from the sunset cut through the mist and the cracked window with an uneasy shimmer. Fred's face was illuminated both by this and the oil lamp that had been placed on a rickety chair in front of him. Also on the chair, neatly arranged by size inside a crumbling leather pouch, was an assortment of blades. Resting upon the floor next to the chair was an axe, grass trimmers, a can of liquid and a small tin. Joseph walked into Fred's field of vision and looked straight at him.

"Mr Darvill. You said we didn't have a ghost so me and Maeve got a plan. We make you the ghost." Fred, barely able to move his lips, spoke. "Huh? I don't understand."

"Most people that become ghosts," replied the male Frostfall, "have had a horrible experience during death. If we make yours as awful and hideous as possible then we have our ghost. Ghost equals a tourist attraction. Tourist attraction means money." After that he walked over to the equipment, Fred struggling and jigging behind him, and from the pouch he took the second smallest blade. Then it was placed to Fred's swollen cheek, below a large bruise, making a series of jagged incisions. Fred tried to pull away and yank the manacles from the wall but only flakes of ancient wallpaper fell. He grunted loudly with pain.

Taking a bigger blade, five more cuts were made on his chest and blood spilled out of the wounds. The captive wailed. By the stairs, Maeve remained impassive and expressionless.

"Please, no,"

"In Salmesbury Hall, one of the ghosts was a priest that was beheaded so…"

The axe that Joseph picked up sliced the bottom of his neck slightly. This made Fred let loose a throaty scream. "But no, too easy. Burning? No, too dangerous. I know! One of the ghosts of Cock Lane was poisoned with arsenic thus…" The tin can on the floor contained a powder. Maeve pried the lips of the dying man apart, scooped out a handful and poured it down his throat.

Then they watched.

One of the bed's rubber wheels squeaked as they moved, reminding Masters of a furiously dripping tap. As they rolled past the other occupants of the ward, he saw that they were as uncomfortable with the noise as he was; they winced and looked at him pityingly, knowing that he was going for surgery before they were. He did not meet their eyes. He had asked if he could walk to his procedure but had been politely but oh-so-firmly told that the insurance carrier for the hospital would not allow it. He had to be pushed like an invalid.

As they reached the end of the ward, Masters saw into the nurses' office. Adrian, his named nurse, saw him and waved reassuringly. Masters managed to raise a hand in weak greeting, but let it fall to the bed almost as soon as he had lifted it. His mouth was dry and the tape around his wedding ring itched.

The porter pushing the bed tried to made conversation as they went into the main corridor, but stopped when he realised that Masters was replying to his questions in non-committal grunts. They moved wordlessly along the bright, airy corridor, past nurses and doctors who did not look at the bed or Masters. He felt like crying out to them – "It might be an everyday thing for you, but it's not for me. I'm going to have surgery. It's not a big operation, but I'm still scared." – but he did not. He kept his mouth clenched firmly shut, trapping the words, along with his fear, inside his throat.

The journey did not take long, perhaps five minutes in all, and Masters was glad when they arrived at a set of double doors. The continual noise from the wheel had become hard to bear, its constant repetition a painful reminder of his own powerlessness. Carefully, the porter eased the bed through the doors and into a small ante-room. Machines lined the wall and faced them as they entered. Shelves looked on impassively, lined with boxes of disposable needles and gloves and other, more mysterious, things. He heard the doors swing shut behind him and looked apprehensively at the other doors set in the wall to his right. Frosted glass panels made it impossible to see what was on the other side of them, but he knew that it must be the operating theatre. A neat sign above the doors read 'Suite One', and a handwritten notice on the wall to their left stated 'Mr. Crighton.'

"Crighton, eh?" said the porter. "He's very quick. I'll be picking you up in ten minutes, you see if I'm not." Masters did not reply.

The porter left when a nurse opened the second set of doors and entered room. In the moment that the doors were open Masters caught a glimpse of clean, white walls and more machinery, before they swung shut, blocking his view once more. The nurse introduced herself cheerfully, saying, "I'm Sandy, and I need to check your details a final time before we carry on." She took the clipboard from the end of the bed and proceeded to ask Masters the same questions about his health and allergies that the nurses on the ward had asked him twice already. She finished by asking, "And you're having a lipoma removed from just below your left shoulder blade?" He replied to all the questions with affirmative noises, not speaking in case his voice cracked with nervousness.

Sandy seemed to sense his anxiety and carried on talking reassuringly as she bustled around the room. She asked questions about his work and his family, not seeming to mind when he did not reply. She lowered the side frames of the bed as she spoke and then helped Masters roll over onto his front. There was an uncomfortable moment when his hospital gown flapped open, revealing his buttocks, but Sandy merely pulled the blankets up and covered him without mentioning it. He supposed she must see things like that all the time. Worse, probably. Finally, she wrapped a blood pressure cuff around his arm and slid a plastic clip over the tip of his right index finger. The clip was attached by a snaking cable to a machine that looked like a computer monitor. Sandy turned on the machine and they both watched speculatively as the display snowed and then came to life. Immediately, the blood pressure cuff began to inflate. Numbers appeared on the display, bright against the black background.

"This here is your heart rate," Sandy said, pointing to a section of the display that read 61.

"And this is the amount of oxygen being carried by your blood." This number was 97. "They're both fine. These bottom numbers are your blood pressure, and that's great too. This top line, the flat one, is where your heartbeat would show, but I've not connected you to the ECG as you're only having a local anaesthetic."

Masters, calmer now, watched the displays with interest. It was odd to be able to see a physical representation of his heart rate, something that he knew instinctively was there but always took for granted. He watched it jump from 61 to 75 and then back down again, and marvelled at such fluctuations. He tried to deliberately alter the number by holding his breath so that his heart might speed up, but it made little difference. The number moved back and forth apparently of its own accord. His oxygen rating was more stable, but even this varied slightly. Eventually, Masters lay still and watched, his head resting on his crossed arms.

"I'll just go and see if they're ready for you," said Sandy and went through to the room beyond. He heard muffled voices and then Sandy was back and removing the cuff and finger clip. She pushed his bed forward.

"Okay, Mr. Masters, Mr. Crighton is ready now," she said cheerily. The bed nosed open the doors ahead of him, which swung back to reveal four gowned figures illuminated by bright sunlight. Through windows set high in the walls Masters could see the most beautiful blue sky, cloudless and everlasting. The walls and polished floor were awash with sunlight. There were more machines lining the walls of this room, which was bigger than the anteroom. Two of the figures were ahead of him, positioned either side of a prominent, blocky piece of equipment, whilst the other two remained on the periphery. One watched him intently whilst the other sat on a chair that looked like a bar stool and leant against a work surface, reading notes on pages tethered in a cardboard file. Masters wondered idly if they were his notes or someone else's.

Ahead of Masters was a space into which Sandy pushed the bed. She came around the front of him, pulled another blood pressure cuff tightly into place and put another clip on his finger, connecting him to the machine directly in front of him. It was covered in labelled dials and gauges, along with the now familiar digital display. Some of the labels he could recognise ('O$_2$', 'Air'), but others consisted of equations and words that he did not recognise. He felt excluded and childlike, as powerless as he had when, as a young man, he had heard his peers talk about things he had not done, places he had not seen.

Surrounded by the evidence of his ignorance, he felt an impotent anger flare within him. A tangle of cables and tubes rested below the machine, held off the floor by metal hooks. Masters' stomach clenched tightly, fear and helplessness struggling for dominance. *This* was why he hated hospitals. He had heard other people talk about the smell or the food or the staff but for Masters, it had always been the sense that something was happening that he was excluded from. Doctors and nurses spoke in codes, did things he could not comprehend, acted in odd ways, became excited about things that seemed, on the face of it, dull. He had always thought that, somehow, medical professionals were a separate breed, another species that had different drives and appetites and desires. They frightened him.

"Now, Mr. Masters, shall we get on?" said Mr

Crighton from his right. He recognised the gentle Scottish lilt and friendly inflections from their meeting earlier in the day.

"Yes," he managed to reply without letting his fear show.

"Firstly, we need to wash your back with antiseptic."

Someone pulled the blanket back from him and his buttocks were exposed again. He had a moment to feel uncomfortable and then he felt the cold sluice of liquid across his skin. He shivered.

"It's a little cold, but don't worry about anything," Crighton said. "I know you're nervous about this, but really, it's a very straightforward procedure." Crighton's calm confidence was contagious, soothing, and Masters felt better. He wanted to ask him to keep talking, to keep soothing him, but dared not. Instead, he managed to say, "Of course, please carry on."

"Now, we'll cover you with towels so you don't get cold and we'll inject you with local anaesthetic." There was the rustle of cloth being unfolded and then the welcome feeling of being covered. He was no longer exposed, except for a square around his left shoulder blade. "You'll feel a scratch and then a stinging sensation as the anaesthetic goes in," said Crighton. "It shouldn't last long, but it will be fairly painful. It's the worst part of the procedure, I promise you."

As he spoke, Crighton was pushing Masters' lipoma around, feeling its shape under the skin and squeezing it gently. Masters had often manipulated it in a similar way himself, reaching over his shoulder and pushing it this way and that, wondering where this hardened lump of subcutaneous fat had come from, why it had chosen to form where it had, why him? He felt a pricking sensation below the lump and then a painful burning. He gritted his teeth, but could not stop an involuntary gasp of pain escaping from his lips. Sandy patted his hand gently and said, "It's horrible, isn't it? It won't last long though. Just a few more seconds." Her hand felt cool and hard. Masters felt another prick and more savage burning which flared brightly before fading away.

There was more muffled talking from behind him and then Masters felt the sting of pain as something cut him. He jerked and gasped. The cutting immediately stopped.

"Is it the pressure you can feel, or does it actually hurt?" asked a woman, to which Masters snapped, "It actually hurts!" He had felt a scalpel cut him. His flesh had been slashed open across his lipoma and it had *hurt*, although it had not been the agony he would have expected. But still, he wasn't supposed to feel *anything*!

"We'll just put some more local in," said Crighton soothingly. Masters braced himself for the stinging, but it never came. Clearly, he was partially numb around his shoulder blade, just not numb *enough*. Perhaps thirty seconds later, the pushing and pulling sensation started again, this time without the attendant pain.

"Does it hurt at all?" asked the woman.

"No," said Masters and let out a breath that he had not realised he was holding. He tried to relax. He rested his head back down on his folded arms with the point of his chin nestled against the back of his hands and looked around without moving. He realised that he could see the reflection of Crighton and his assistant, presumably the woman, in the highly polished glass and metal of the machine in front of him. He watched for a minute or two, feeling an almost guilty pleasure, as though he was privy to something that should have remained private.

The figures looked twisted and deformed in the glass fascia, stretched out like vultures of tendon and fabric, their limbs strangely elongated and birdlike as they picked at his back. He tried to associate the movements he could see with the sensations he could feel, but could not. Eventually, he had to turn his head as the figures began to hold up pieces of bloody cloth and at one point a glinting scalpel. Memories of hospital documentaries flooded his mind, of stretched skin and sundered flesh, and he began to feel nauseous.

After an indeterminate length of time, Mr. Crighton said brightly, "There! I told you that it would shell out easily, didn't I? That looks perfectly normal, Mr. Masters, and I don't think you've anything to worry about. We'll just stitch you up now and then you can go back to the ward." He voice was thick and heavy, although he sounded cheerful, as if he had just received good news. Masters sighed in relief and let his gaze wander.

More pushing and pulling at his back. Masters carried on looking to the side, avoiding the reflections in the machine. Sandy appeared in his vision, carrying a small jar which she placed on the work surface. Inside the jar, something floated in cloudy liquid – a yellowy, bulbous object flecked with darker patches of blood. He stared at it, startled, unsure of how to feel about seeing his lump displayed to him in this way. The crenellated surface reminded him unpleasantly of a brain and he turned away thinking, *That was inside me. I've moved that around with my fingers and pushed it hoping it would go away without me having to be cut.* It looked sad and unhealthy, alone in its glass jar.

Rather than look at the jar again, Masters looked up at the display. His blood pressure and oxygen rates had fallen, but his pulse rate was elevated. He was determined that his fear of hospitals and doctors would not cause him to make a fool of himself here. He tried to clamp down on the hypochondria that told him his changed blood pressure and heart rate were indicative of some more serious problem. As he watched, his pulse rate leapt again, up into the early nineties. He felt his heart, a wild beat in his chest that sent vibrations along his whole body.

In desperation, Masters looked again at the

rest of the machine ahead of him. Closer to him than the dials and gauges, he focused on the reflections. He saw the room behind him. He saw Crighton and the female assistant, bent low over his back – odd, inhuman shapes that seemed stretched, twisted. And then he saw what they were doing, the way their arms and heads darted up and down and the way that they picked at his flesh and how they were slathering over him. He saw fingers twisted into claws and dark, gaping mouths.

Without thinking, Masters bucked and thrashed on the table, the instinct to flee overcoming all rational thought. He felt the scalpel bite deep into his flesh as he arched back against it, hearing shrieks rich with anger and something else, something less definable. A terrible wanting. A *hunger.* And then he was off the bed and crashing to the floor, screaming as he fell.

Happy Families

The trio woke in a room panelled with shiny white tiles. Above, a single pulsating light lit the room up as brightly as a floodlit football pitch, gleaming and intense and allowing no shadows to manifest. The air was humid and all three of them had a glistening layer of sweat over their skin. The Castle family were each on a metal-framed bed with mattresses that felt like bricks. Under the bright light were Bill Castle, PhD (Father), Gillian 'Jill' Castle (Mother), and Oli (Son). None of them knew where they were, or why, or how they got there. Had they even chosen to go there?

Jill swung her legs out of the bed and found herself dressed in an oversized ivory-coloured gown, like one you might find hospital patients wearing, or a kimono but with tighter sleeves.

She didn't remember owning such an item but knew she did not like it. It didn't feel right. The outfit itched around the shoulders and clamped her arms.

Oli also extricated his legs from underneath the bed sheets then stared at his mum. Like her, he was wearing the same type of ivory outfit. He did not feel instantly frightened but he was disoriented, his mind prone to assuming the current part of life was just an unusual adventure even if he didn't understand it. The seven-year old did know he detested the gown because it itched greatly. Oli pulled a sleeve up then scratched his arm. He tried to speak but only a croak sounded from his aching throat. He tried again and failed once more. Oli decided a third try would be pointless.

Bill felt groggy. He took his time clambering out from under the bed sheets. They felt like they were rubber or plastic, sticky, clammy and uncomfortable. Unnatural, like they didn't belong. He rubbed his forehead and he found himself wanting to clutch it. His head wouldn't clear and the harder he thought, the louder was the stab of pain emanating, it felt like, from his skull. In an effort to ignore the pain, Bill gazed around the blurry room. His vision had just about returned but the odd patch was still distorted and out of focus. The chamber appeared to be a perfect, upright cylinder. Bill noticed his wife and, like his son, made an attempt to speak which, again like his son, failed. The clothing he wore was slightly different from that of his wife and child. As well as the gown he also wore a belt, as if to suggest that his belly was too large for the garment. *A bit cheeky*, he thought.

Oli jumped down to the floor and began to examine things in the room, his childish curiosity kicking in. His delicate, small hands caressed the tiles. They felt cold, like freezer drawers. The material of the ivory gown must have been very thin; the chill pressed against his skin as if the gown were not there. He didn't find the floor interesting.

As Oli stood, a voice bellowed around the chamber from an unknown source.

"HELLO CASTLES. I AM THE HOST. YOU DO NOT KNOW ME. I WILL RETURN SOON. UNTIL THEN, GOODBYE."

The adults heard the voice, but only barely registered what The Host was saying. The meaning of the words was jumbled, piling onto their state of confusion. When their son enquired croakily, his voice finally returning, what the mysterious voice was or said they could only answer with uncertainty. Now their voices seemed to be coming back too but they still did not sound right, their words jumbled and overlapping like they'd forgotten how to speak and would have to readjust to it, like a young child getting used to phonetics, something they would later find easy.

As they adjusted to their new surroundings and tried to work out what was going on, the Castles each tried to think but there was something wrong in each of them, something in their heads. Like a burglar in their home, only a burglar who was about to take an item but couldn't do it until a switch was flicked. The almost-burglar, if you will.

Bill stood up and felt along the wall. It was smooth with no cracks and no panels that could hide the thing that would grant them release to the world beyond. Not a hidden panel or camouflaged doorknob. Nothing. It didn't occur to them they might not want to see what lay outside their confines.

"HELLO AGAIN. I WOULD LIKE A BIT MORE ACTION FROM YOU. IT IS NECESSARY. YOU ARE SUPPOSED TO BE MY TEST SUBJECTS. LET ME GET YOU STARTED."

The voice ceased quickly, emanating from everywhere and then nowhere, yet nothing seemed to happen. Or that's what they thought.

The light above them started to flash. It was slow at first, pulsating at six times a minute, increasing to seven.

Bill continued to feel, prodding and poking the wall. He moved completely around the room, looking under the steel beds and probing every surface. His wife was comforting her son, reassuring him that things were okay, keeping his attention away from the things around him and trying to stop any worries he might have. Bill stood up and walked over to the pair and took a seat. Suddenly, he felt something drifting out of his gown and saw it settle on the floor. He didn't know what it was. Jill picked it up and was halfway through passing it back to Bill when her arm stopped moving. Her eyes were transfixed on the picture. Her mouth opened and closed a couple of times and then she began to speak.

"Bill, who's this?" she asked, then hesitantly passed him the paper. It was a photo of Bill with another woman. It could have been from any time – the 80s, the 70s – but unfortunately for Bill, a date and sentence had been written in the top corner: *20/10/19 – Don't tell the other Mrs.* Jill's mouth opened and a tear welled in the corner of her eye.

"Bill, answer me." Suddenly a wafer of information launched into his brain; the metaphorical burglar had just become an attacker. Bill suddenly remembered a memory he felt he shouldn't have. It was him with another woman. Her name though...was it Sally Anne...or Mary Anne? Other sudden pieces of knowledge stabbed into his mind – her name was Sally Anne, age 30, Catholic, virgin. Of those facts he was immediately certain. *But how?* She looked pretty in the picture and Bill found himself looking at her more often than he should. He didn't know what to say but then a sentence was launched onto the tip of his tongue, flexing to form a sentence: "I'm seeing

her, Jill. I love her. At least more than I love you."
Shut up! Stop! Why say that?

Jill's mouth froze. Her son was oblivious and assumed they were having a different conversation. Voices weren't raised. Yet. Ignorance maybe was bliss. But how wrong was the boy, oh so very wrong.

The pulsating had increasing to fifteen times a minute.

Jill did not seem to question his answer as quickly, stuttering and waiting, then suddenly she responded rapidly, "Seeing someone... fucking adulterer! Motherfucker!" The wife got to her feet. "Well who is she? A whore? A common shit you found on the street? Am I not good enough? In fact, have I ever been good enough?" Oli did not know what was going on but he knew he wanted to intervene.

"Mum. Dad. Please stop," he meekly interjected.

"Oli, darling. Let me and Mum talk for a few moments." Bill was now standing also.

"Don't speak to him. Fucker! You bastard!" She went to slap him but he moved out the way just in time, allowing only her sharp wedding ring to scratch his face, creating a small cut. Bill lifted his hand gently and felt the cut. When he drew back his hand a smear of drops was on his fingers. Blood dribbled down under his left eye and stained the kimono. Jill took off her emerald engagement ring and hurled it on the ground next to the drops of red, the blood standing out like a single star in a blank sky.

"Mummy, Daddy please—" Oli spoke, trying to intervene. The son did not know why his parents were arguing.

"Shut up, Oli." Her whole perception of her seven-year old changed. She slapped him across the face with one clean swing. *That'd teach him to be so rude. The childish shit.* That slap caused Oli to stagger back slightly then tears began to roll down his cheeks. They splashed onto the white tiles and mixed with the blood. Oli did not like being hurt. Mummy or Daddy had never hurt him before. What had he done to deserve that? Oli could sense something was wrong, without having to concentrate on the cause of the argument. Something was so wrong. He looked up. Oli hated the light. The light was wrong. The light was bad. The light was hurting him, his mum and his dad.

Everything was about to get a whole lot worse.

In a flash, a memory was launched into Jill's mind and simultaneously landed in Bill's also. She'd gambled over ten grand down the drain without winning a single penny. Ten bloody, motherfucking grand! And then spent another three grand on alcohol. The bills and credit cards had still not been cleared and nor were they likely to be in the near future. All in one year. Bill frowned and his brain twisted, a new side – be it a metaphorical burglar gaining entry,or one always there but hidden – emerged into full, blossoming view.

Bill approached his wife and spat that issue at her: "I'm bad hmmm? But it's okay for you to slap Oli? Or waste thirteen grand?" Jill realised her action and tried to cover it, muttering "Heat of the moment" and "That's over now". Bill clenched his fist and punched her cheek. Jill threw up her arms but she was too slow to block the blow. The force was massively, unnaturally powerful. It sent her back onto the bed, in a bedraggled starfish shape, bleeding from her mouth and nose. She let out a blood-curdling scream.

Bravely, Oli got to his feet, tears staining his cheeks, and, with his entire might, screamed at the parents who looked like they were about to tear each other apart. Bill, like his wife previously, flung his hand at Oli, sending him sprawling onto the floor. The man hardly noticed this, registering it as a reflex rather than conscious or deliberate action. This was about to break into carnage.

"HELLO MY FRIENDS. GOOD TO SEE YOU ARE STILL AT IT. I JUST CAME TO SAY HELLO. OH AND YOU KNOW YOU WANT TO DO IT. FIGHT! FIGHT! KILL! KILL!"

Twenty-three pulsations a minute.

The words and light began to take effect almost immediately. Oli had a nosebleed, which added another layer of blood to the tiles and sent spatters up the wall. Neither parent cared though. Their horn-locking was all they could focus on. The air was becoming thick with anger and the smell of sweat and blood. Bill sent his fist towards her head, but Jill dodged, sending a knee into his stomach and then dropping it down into his groin. Bill managed to avoid the worst of the attack and met it with one of his own. He ripped the front of her gown, revealing a small fraction of her naked chest.

Thirty-two pulsations a minute.

Oli was crawling around the floor, his vision beginning to blur. In a desperate action he flung himself with unnatural power at his mother, who tumbled backwards back onto the bed just as she was getting up. Bill threw his son aside and kneeled over his victimised wife. Pleads and insults filled the air from both parent and child alike. Bill had loosened his belt, drawing it away from his waist and was using it to whip his wife. *The woman will submit,* he thought. *She must do.* That was her duty. Metal buckle and all, the weapon scarred her face. Her upper gown was ripped at the front, as were her attacker's lower gown and shoulders. Battered, Bill drove a fist into her exposed flesh, landing it just underneath her left breast. Another punch was hammered in to her stomach. These injuries each caused tiny trickles of blood, and would form massive bruises. She clawed at his arm, drawing lines that wept blood. Bill twisted her arm back but was interrupted by a lump thrusting itself into his arm. The lump, Oli, was almost knocked aside but clung on. His teeth dug into the man's skin. Bill repeatedly slammed his arm against the white tiles until his offspring slumped to the floor. Now, Oli ceased to move.

Heartbeats filled the ears of the two remaining, charged by pulsations.

Everyone and everything was drenched. Blood, sweat, tears.

The adrenalin-fuelled couple were battling with each other. Injuries were constantly being expanded or reopened. Jill launched herself out of the way and grabbed her husband's arm with her bloodied hands. He overpowered his wife though. Menacingly, the man towered above her, huge over her small body. He pounced upon her like a fat panther and wrestled with her. She was forced to the floor. Jill was now fighting for every single breath she could muster. His knee dug into her stomach and she regurgitated a sickly red mess, spitting it all over Bill. This enraged him even more and he delivered a karate chop to her sensitive areas. She let loose a mottled cry of torment, sending her writhing. Bill – the Bill she'd entered the cylinder with – was no longer there, only his body was. His soul had abandoned him. She was grasping for breath, spasming slightly. One hand on her neck, Bill was twisting his belt into a noose with his other hand. The makeshift noose looped around her neck and Bill yanked as hard as he could, his right foot against her back, and her neck pulled back as far he could stretch the belt. Coughs echoed faintly around the room. Her husband's belt strained harder. She could feel the burning of her neck collapsing. Finally, her eyes started to glaze over. Surprisingly quickly, her body slumped and she had nothing left, no fight, no breath. No life. Bill stood up and gazed at the light.

Forty-five pulsations a minute.

The room was red. He was red. It was all red. Bloody red.

"WELL NOW. I SUPPOSE IT'S TIME FOR SUBJECTS 19 AND 20 TO BE TESTED THEN."

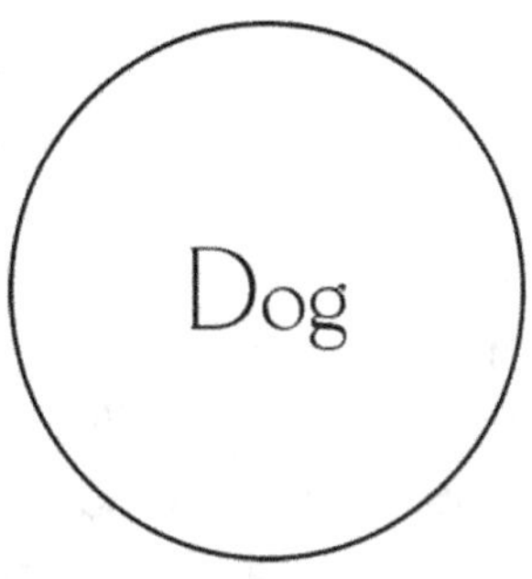

Grit scraped its way under the skin of his palms. He grunted, his knees taking the shock a moment later and then the crack of the closing door over-rode the pain and he looked over his shoulder, knowing already what he was going to see.

In the concrete wall the door's outline was as thin as button thread – up, across, down – and featureless as a frosted puddle. He stood, barely noticing the peeled skin hanging from his hands and went to the wall. Running his fingertips across the blank expanse, he found the edge between the door and the jam maddeningly too thin to get even his nails into. Swearing to himself, he stepped back. He was here, it seemed, until someone let him out. Letting himself fall back against the wall, he slid down into a sitting position, knees drawn up in front of him, hands held in to his body. Sliding had pulled his shirt out from his trousers and the wall was rough against his back.

At his front, the room stretched out, its floor scattered with blocks of choppily carved or cast stone. Above, the ceiling was high, out of reach. Everything was grey, glistening with damp. Apart from the blocks, the only features were a series of jutting pipes or tubes around the rim of the room where the walls kissed the ceiling, and a drain in the floor, a rusted metal lattice perhaps a foot in length on each side. He rose gingerly, pain rippling out from both knees, and went to it. From between the metal bars, a shaft peered back at him. An experimental pull revealed that the lattice was set solid into the surrounding floor; pulling left rusted streaks across his scored palms, beneath which he could see grains of stone impacted up under the skin on the pads of his hands. They throbbed when he thought about them. He tried not to think.

Something hard and cold hit him between his shoulders. He staggered, his leg cracking against one of the blocks and then he fell, his shoulder battering into the rough floor. He rolled, expecting further attack, but nothing came. He sat, gasping at the movement, and looked around. Water. There was water spattering across the floor and spilling around his back and shoulders. Looking up, he saw one of the tubes, its end dripping. Had they sprayed water at him?

Who were 'they'?

Carefully, he rolled his trouser leg up. Below the grazed kneecap, a fresh tear in his skin was leaking blood, the nerve-endings yelping as cold air and colder water touched against them. Thick, clear fluid had already started to ooze from its edges along with the blood. Grit, black and grey, was impacted into the raw flesh and threads of material from his trousers were twined around its ragged edges. He was picking one of the threads away, wincing as it came, pulling the exposed skin forward, when another jet of water hit him.

This one was warmer and weaker, breaking across his chest and waist. He started as it hit him, bracing himself for worse but it did not come. The water died away to nothing, leaving him in a widening pool of liquid that gathered, sending questing fingers towards the grid. He did not move, but stayed on the floor. Water dripped from his arms and face, growing colder and drawing out gooseflesh from his skin. What madness was this? What Hell was happening here? Water? Blocks of stone in concrete rooms? He drew his leg up to him, pressing the ugly wound in the hope that it might stop bleeding. It did not.

After he did not know how many minutes, he stood. His leg felt weak, unable to bear its normal weight, and he found himself limping as he walked around the edge of the room, looking for some clue as to what was going on, some idea of how he might get out. Apart from the doorway, flush into the wall and as unassailable as sacred flesh, there seemed no other exit. An experimental tap against the door hurt his knuckles, more grazes to add to his growing collection, and the sound revealed a solid thing set in its immovability. God *damn. Fuck* damn!

Another spray of water hit him, this one scalding. He lurched to escape it, his leg wobbling dangerously and his already bruised shoulder banging into the wall. The sandpaper caress of the stone licked at him, lubricated by water and fear. What the fuck, the *fuck*, was going on here?

Sounds came to him now. There was a distant clanking, a noise like air trapped in a radiator. More of the nozzles set around the ceiling were beginning to drip and they reminded him uncomfortably of snake fangs, swollen and dribbling venom. As he looked around, one of the nozzles bucked, firing a stream of water with pinpoint accuracy into his face. Thinner than the previous jets, this one was hard and cold and stung. He shook his head, doglike, to clear the water from his eyes and fringe and then another spray hit him, low and precise on his injured leg, less powerful but more painful as it battered at the raw, flayed flesh. He screamed then, as much from fury and terror as pain, and tried to hobble away but wherever he went in the room, the water followed him. When he crouched low behind one of the stone blocks, jets came from behind; when he pressed himself against the wall, they came from the side or opposite, fast and vicious and on target. Water flowed across the cold concrete and around the blocks before spilling over the lip of the drain and falling into the darkness. Drips of his blood fell sometimes, merging pink with the water before fading to nothing, diluting and spreading in the trickle and flow. Bruises flowered on his skin where the floor or walls had beaten at him, nestling amongst red marks etched by the harsher sprays or the finer jets. Written across his flesh was the record of his imprisonment, the story of his time in this room.

There seemed no reason or logic to the sprays, no consistency. Cold, hot, lukewarm, thin, fat, harsh, gentle, the only things they shared in common was their existence and their homing in on him. Except... except... gradually, he began to think that there was a pattern to them, some design in the spacing between the sprays, some hidden regularity. Some gaps were shorter, some longer, but there seemed a rhythm to it, one he could almost grasp, could feel teasing at his fingertips. There was structure here, but what?

Eventually, even terror and pain faded, melting into a blurring whole. What *was* this place? Why had he been brought here?

Where *was* 'here'? He tried to remember the time before 'here', but could not. There was something in his mind about a struggle, a capture, but whose? His? Was he the abductee, or the abductor? And why this place, and why the water? He called out, shouting loud to the emotionless ceiling, but the only response he received was more sprays, hot and cold and sharp and dull, hitting his face. Eventually, he stopped calling. He was thirsty, and the irony of his thirst made him laugh. Surrounded by water, and yet he was forced to cup his hands against his chest to catch drips, raise them to his mouth and lick at them with a tongue that felt thick and cracked. Again, he teased at his memory, looking for an explanation, but none came. The concrete walls and stone blocks, impassive, watched as he wandered around his prison. He wanted to scream, to beat the walls, to be violent, beg for his life, but he did not. There seemed little point; here was simply water and solitude.

Eventually, he sat on one of the blocks, slumping over so that his hair hung down and his face was at least partially protected from the constant spray. Still they came, first one side then the other, now scalding and now almost ice. Water pooled around his feet, chilling his toes. The material of his trousers was heavy and waterlogged, dragging at the skin of his thighs when he shifted. He could feel grit under his soles, its tiny edges digging and plucking at him. His wounds ached and bled, still raw and unable to start their healing. Every time a scab began to form, its sticky accretion was torn away by the pummelling water, indelicate fingers wresting at the flesh and poking at the ragged edges of skin. Fear and pain seemed to have peaked and receded, as though his body could not maintain their upkeep. His muscles trembled, the uncontrollable shivers rocking his body like that of a palsied old man.

Another jet of water hit him in the centre of his back, but this one was different. Instead of coming and going rapidly, it started soft and stayed, growing in strength. The pressure soon meant that he had to tense his body to prevent himself from being pushed over, and then to actively push back against the spray. It was as though someone had trained a firehose on him, was urging it to greater and greater power to push him off the block. Surrounded by a fury of water vapour and battered flesh, the sound of liquid-ripped air loud in his ears, he arched himself back, determined to stay upright.

And then the water was gone.

Overbalancing, he fell back. Twisting, he

caught at the block, scrabbling at the stone, his nails tearing and bending. Another jet hit him hard from the front, tilting him further. Another jet. Another, and he was gone, splashing to the floor and hitting his forehead with a crack that he heard rather then felt. Water, cold and solid, bubbled up his nostrils as he inhaled in surprise, hitting the back of his throat and dripping into his lungs. He coughed, a tearing that jerked his whole body and made his aches blossom in sympathy. Water and mucus sprayed out from his nose and spattered down his lips as tears were forced from his eyes. His lungs seemed closed, tightened and bound by unseen barbs and he coughed again, harder and sharper. The cough turned into a retch, spasms wracking him as his stomach and chest convulsed and clenched. He vomited, a thin stream of bile-flavoured water spattering out from his mouth and coating his teeth with its thickening taste and then he was done and exhausted and spent.

There was a click.

He rolled over onto his back and sat up in time to see the door slip back into its frame and shut with a dull, final sound. Wheezing, he rose on unsteady legs and lurched to the wall, banging his fists against the uncaring stone and letting his body fall against the barred exit. He screamed then, tears of anger and frustration merging with the water and spittle on his cheeks and chin, crying in terror and fear and desperation and wanting, *wishing*, that this would end.

Something banged into his leg. Startled, he leapt back as another fucking jet of water, this one warm and weak, hit him in the side of the head. His vision, already blurred, swayed as the liquid splashed across his face and he could see nothing for a moment. Blinking, he tried to clear his eyes and look around. The room stretched around him as before, a grey expanse that glinted and glimmered with a sheen of reflecting, cold liquid. It was just the room, but the room with a difference. A shadow cowered in the far corner, small and wretched and shivering.

There was a dog in the corner.

He threaded his way through the blocks towards it, trying to see it properly when another spray hit him, this one low and cold. When it had gone, he carried on. Closer to, he saw that the dog was a mongrel, its fur tufted and patched black and brown. Its tail was down, shivering between its back legs and it growled at him as he approached, its lips pulling back from teeth that gleamed white and gums that were pale with fear or shock or both. Its threat display was absurd, he thought, the actions of a small and frightened thing making itself appear bigger. He crouched, holding one hand out to the creature, making low crooning noises in his throat and muttering half-formed words of comfort. The dog growled more fiercely, its dark eyes darting above its snarls. Still he held his hand out, still he coaxed. He had no idea why, but it was important that he comfort the dog. Company, possibly, or to reassert his own humanity in a situation that seemed bereft of warmth. He saw the dog's defences begin to drop, heard its growls start to tail off, and then the water hit.

A blast caught him on his head, stinging his ear, whilst another hit the dog squarely in its side. It yelped and leapt forwards, snapping at his outstretched hand savagely and darting past him. It ran around the room, its howls coming back from the walls as muffled echoes. The cacophony was awful, the noises seeming to come from all sides at once and he groaned at this new assault. The dog, having made a full circle of the room, was approaching him. It looked as though it was about to attack, but veered off at the last moment, contenting itself with a bark and a half-hearted snap at his leg. Growing more frenzied, it dashed between the blocks in the centre of the room, its tail low to the floor. Strings of drool hung from its lips, slather that swung and jerked as it ran and yelped. He watched the dog warily, following it with his eyes and moving as little as possible, as it ran and ran and ran until it had worn itself out. Finally, it cowered in a corner, keening when water hit it.

The sprays came, again and again. He stayed on the other side of the room from the dog, letting the water hit him whenever it came. His skin became tender, as though it was sunburned, prickling against anything that touched it. Their accuracy and randomness meant he could not avoid the sprays: he wished they were not so changeable. But, he remembered, they were not; not totally. He concentrated, letting his mind move away from his flesh and into its own place. He thought and he waited. His own sense of precision, of order, had set the pace of his own life, and he set it free now to see what order it could find.

Eventually, he began to detect a rhythm to the sprays, a regularity not in the attacks themselves but in their timing. Exhausted, he sat on one of the smoother blocks, shivering with cold and a tiredness that felt as though it had settled into his very bones, and began to count. As he did so, he watched the dog, It was growing frantic again, running in tight circles as it tried as helplessly as he had to escape the water. Its fur hung in bedraggled clumps and its eyes were wide and white. It teeth, set into gums as pale as marble, looked huge. He was worried about it; at the moment, it was ignoring everything in its attempts to escape, but if it chose to attack, he did not know if he had the strength to defend himself. He carried on watching, its scurried loops oddly hypnotic, as the rhythm of this place revealed itself to him.

As far as he could tell, the attacks came according to set times; he counted them using the child's 'Mississippi' game. There was a seventy second gap, a twenty five second one, a forty second one, a fifty second one, a ten second one, and twenty second one and then back to the seventy second one. He counted through the pattern three times; each time the same, as far as he could judge. Water dripped from him, gathering around his buttocks and trickling to the floor. The drain mouth sucked hungrily at it, its hollow-throated swallows chuckling lightly between the sprays.

He counted through the pattern again, twice, a third time, into a fourth, letting the first, longer gaps pass by without moving. He tried to relax, to get into the centred state he used before any physical activity. He counted fifty seconds and then let the water hit him, this one a hot spurt in the centre of his back. Now, to count with meaning. *One Mississippi two Mississippi three Mississippi four Mississippi five Mississippi* and he let his muscles prepare *six Mississippi seven Mississippi* his legs pulled back and his heels braced back against the block *eight Mississippi nine Mississippi* he leaned forward *ten Missi—* and he jumped.

He felt the spray of water scythe the air behind him as he fell to his hands and knees on the floor, old water splashing up around legs and arms as new water arced over his back and spattered harmlessly on the floor beyond him. He crawled rapidly forwards, coming up into a triumphant leap as the spray finished. They had missed! He howled, a wordless shout of exultation for an obscure, almost certainly pointless victory. Hearing him, the dog began to bark again, becoming more and more frenzied as he continued to shout, punching the air and jumping as he did so. He had taken back some tiny splinter of control, had stopped being a prisoner for the shortest moment and become an individual who could make choices, could influence things, and it felt wonderful.

There was a click, and the part of his brain that had continued to count, was still timing the gaps, told him to expect the water again, but it did not come. Instead, the next spray concentrated entirely on the dog, dousing it with liquid which shimmered vibrantly in the subdued light. The dog howled and began to shake itself, running in wild, tight circles and crashing into the wall without apparent care. Falling silent, he watched, astounded. What was this? What was happening here?

What was that smell?

Petrol. The dog was covered in petrol. Even as

the realisation hit, there was another click, a spark of yellow in the grey surroundings, and then a fireball, greasy with burning hair and flesh, exploded in the corner of the room.

The dog's cries grew louder and higher as the flames swallowed it. At the centre of the inferno, he could see a moving shadow that thrashed in a spastic, bitter dance. It leapt and capered, staggering between the blocks towards him and then away again, rolling as it fell and then coming up into another swaying movement. The air filled with the stench of roasting fat, of hair shrivelling and blackening, of skin puckering and splitting and peeling, of tooth enamel cracking, of lips blackening and contracting.

Of the dog, dying.

He tried to scoop water off the floor and throw it at the poor creature, but it was hopeless. What little he could gather hit the flames and simply hissed into steam. The heat thrust heavy arms at him, a sinuous, invisible thing that was as effective a barrier as a wall or a locked door. Eventually he retreated, gagging on the smell and the taste of burning animal that laced the air. He watched as the creature finally slumped against the wall and the flames died away to tiny blue things that licked at its charred and ravaged flesh. Its legs twitched and a last, miserable sound escaped from its throat and then it was still.

Burnt flesh floated towards the drain at the centre of the room, catching in the grate before falling away into the blackness. Steam, its rich aroma catching in his nostrils, coated his skin and formed a cowl around his head. The rainbow patterns of petrol gleamed over the surface of the water, nestling against pieces of dog as they drifted away from its carcass.

Another jet of water hit him. Another. Another. *Another.*

Eventually, he rose and started to wander aimlessly around the perimeter of the room. He avoided the dog, stepping gingerly around its corpse, and was horrified to feel that the water pooled around it was warm, gentler on the soles of his feet than the liquid that lay around the rest of the room. He wanted to stay near it, steal some of it warmth, but could not. The warmth was its life, carried away and cooling even as he walked on.

At the door, he stopped. He let his fingers

trail around the barely perceptible ridge where it met the frame, hoping for a place to grip, a place to take the strain, a place to *pull*. Nothing. It was flush and solid. No tears, he told himself. Get angry, not upset. Get angry and get out.

But how? This place was like an egg, inverted, trapping him like some helpless bird. *Why me,* he wondered, slumping onto a block. *Why me and not some other poor bastard? I'm nobody. I've not made any enemies, I haven't hurt anyone or killed anyone, I haven't cheated or robbed anyone. It doesn't make sense. I don't even know where this place is, who brought me here, why I'm here. And that poor dog died because I thought I'd done something to beat whoever it was that's doing this to me. Some pointless victory, avoiding a water jet.* As if on cue, another stream of liquid sprayed against his side. He winced as it prodded his bruised flesh. Looking down, he saw it swirling around his feet and running across his bare toes. The light reflecting across the surface of the water created distorted, fractured images, reminding him of the pieces of burnt dog being harried away from the creature's carcass by the flow. His breath hitched in his chest. *No,* he told himself. *No tears.*

He did not realise that the door was moving

until it had swung inwards a few inches. Startled, he watched as it opened fully and then jumped towards the entrance with a yelp of joy.

Something punched him viciously in the chest, and carried on punching. He felt himself driven back from the doorway. The pressure and pain in his chest swelled and he stumbled. He had a brief glimpse of figures in the doorway, two of them holding down the heavy hosepipe that spat at him, controlling it and keeping it aimed at him. Its bite shifted as he fell, dancing around from his chest to his back as he twisted, pinning him to the floor. The pressure was terrible. His head cracked against one of the blocks and blood like cheap melting chocolate began to drip down onto the floor. His hand splashed into it, disrupting its journey to the drain. More pain, indistinguishable from the rest, crept across his fragile flesh, hooking itself to his muscles and bones. He wondered if the figures intended to crush him with the water from the hose, and then tears came, unbidden and unwanted. What the fuck was happening to him? What the fuck was going on? What insanity was this, that he was to be killed by water at the behest of people he did not know?

The pressure of the hose leapt, beat at his shoulders and then glanced across the back of his head. Driven forwards, his head cracked again into the block and another spray of blood escaped from him, sending scattered droplets out like seeds. He cried out, shrieking against his captors and the water and what was happening to him. Misery and terror tore at his throat, screeching, living things that pulsed in his wounds and spattered in the water around him.

And then, as suddenly as it had begun, the spray stopped. The sound of it, he realised, had been loud and now the silence lay against him with a weight of equal volume. He felt light, as though he could float up against the air like a punctured, ripped bag. Even his pain was light, throbbing with his heartbeat and sending his blood out from a myriad tears and grazes. He groaned as he pulled himself up to his knees, his limbs trembling. Dizziness rippled through him, making him stagger, and he put out a hand to steady himself. There was something in his mouth, something hard. He spat; fragments of teeth clattered against the block, their porcelain clink muted by the strings of bloodied saliva that cocooned them. His tongue found the hole in his gum and poked it as he sat on the block. A molar, gone.

He was too tired even to cry now. He let himself slump over, resting his head in his hands. Through his laced fingers, he looked around the room that had become his prison. Was this Hell? Limbo? Was he being tortured for information that he did not know if he possessed? In the name of *fuck*, what was this?

Something dark moved at the periphery of his vision. He looked up, his body tensing in case of another attack with the hose. Nothing happened.

The dark thing moved again, a large shape that darted from block to block. Oh, Christ, what was this?

The second dog, its fur already wet, began to howl.

This is a transcript of the audio log recorded by the operator on duty at Security Lodge 13 on the night of the incident. The recordings were made as per usual procedure to the Asylum Record System every 15 minutes, at the Dewers' Institute for the Criminally Insane on the night of 13th April 2011, and they remain the only evidence available as to the occurrences of that night. Whether it helps to determine what happened is a matter for the reader to decide.

<u>Night Shift Log April 13th, 2013</u>

Guard on duty, Security Lodge 13:
David Jones

Shift start time: 12.30 a.m.

<u>Inmates</u>
<u>(recorded at start of shift)</u>

Corridor A, Cell 1:
Samantha Ingleberry, 19
Corridor A, Cell 2:
Johnny Pollard Seymour, 76
Corridor A, Cell 3:
Carol Johnson, 50
Corridor A, Cell 4:
Theresa Juarez, 45
Corridor A, Cell 5:
William Charleston, 35
Corridor A, Cell 6:
Derek Mills, 89
Corridor A, Cell 7:
Sally Gorse, 38
Corridor B, Cell 1:
Sylvester Darabont, 55
Corridor B, Cell 2:
Grace Hosmer-Angel, 92
Corridor B, Cell 3:
Joseph Grimesy, 64
Corridor B, Cell 4:
Moira Sutton, 33
Corridor B, Cell 5:
Francis Sebastian Withenshawe, 21
Corridor B, Cell 6:
Ferdinand Sykes, 31

1:00   Sutton is getting aggressive and
       is demanding guard Diana Worbeck
       set her free otherwise she will
       get another prisoner to rape
       them. Incident recorded.

1:15   Guard Riley Hope isn't
        responding after going into
        Corridor A to investigate a
        minor disturbance. I will send
        James Suthersfield from the
        guard room to investigate.

1:30   Guard Suthersfield isn't
        responding to my calls either
        after going to investigate. No
        sign of either man on the
        cameras.

1:45   Security cameras in Corridor A
        are non-functional. I can now
        not check on cells A1 - A7.
        Have reported problem to our
        technicians.

2:00   Technicians are hoping to
        arrive at 4:45 to repair the
        cameras but that time could
        vary depending on traffic.

2:15   I have just received a report
        from an unknown source saying
        that Gorse has escaped and
        overpowered 2 guards with a
        makeshift knife.

2:30   Withenshawe has also escaped,
        along with Mills. I can hear
        them shouting in the corridor.
        Someone is screaming.

2:45   Five more guards have been
        called to assist and detain
        the escaped inmates. I have
        completely sealed off the
        Security Lodge.

3:00   Mills has been detained and
        put back in his cell but Gorse
        and Withenshawe are still at
        large.

3:15   The other inmates are
        extremely rowdy and are
        attempting to force their
        cells open. Guard Hope has
        appeared back on the security
        cameras but he is almost
        unrecognisable. He seems to
        have been mutilated. This
        could be a problem with the
        camera feed but I have phoned
        an ambulance and told them to
        be here quickly. Amanda
        Billington has left the guard
        room to assist. This action
        has been reported. I have
        requested back up however
        radios are non-functional.
        Alarm systems are also not
        working.

3:30   There are two bodies on the
        floor of Corridor B. They have
        been mutilated to such a

degree that I cannot tell who
they are.

3:45   There are, as far as I can
        tell, only 4 or 5 guards still
        alive. I shall arm myself and,
        if   necessary,   leave   the
        Security Lodge in an attempt
        to escape.

4:00   Inmate   Sykes   is   crawling
        through the ventilation shaft.
        He entered in Corridor B and I
        believe he will aim to reach
        here.

4:15   As per my prediction, Sykes
        came here but I disabled him
        with a chair.

4:30   All   security   cameras   are   now
        shut   down.   A   few   are   still
        relaying the noises and sounds
        from   the   asylum.   There   are
        screams and moans.

4:45   Guards are not responding and
        from the sounds on the cameras
        more prisoners have escaped. I
        will remain strong and pray.

5:00   The main lights have shut down
        and emergency lights have come
        on. I have activated emergency
        protocols   and   am   currently

attempting to get the security
cameras back online. Currently,
it is in vain.

5:15   At least three inmates are
        immediately outside the
        Security Lodge. They are
        trying to gain access by
        forcing the doors. So far the
        doors are holding. I have, as
        a precaution, made a makeshift
        barrier and placed it against
        the door.

5:30   Sykes has disappeared from where
        I left him. I can't see him in
        the room but I can still hear
        his rasping breaths. Oh god.

5:45   The technicians that I sent
        for have not made contact. I
        can only assume they have been
        killed by the inmates or they
        have not arrived.

6:00   The security cameras have come
        back online but I don't think
        it is the technicians because
        of a message appearing on all
        screens: *SURRENDER TO THE
        INMATES OR FOR THE SECOND TIME
        WE WILL OVERRUN THE ASYLUM.*

6:15   The inmates have almost gained
        access. I am going to remain

vigilant. I do not understand the message so I hope it is a problem with the system or a message from one of the inmates' profiles.

6:30   The banging on the door has stopped and I can't hear any noise on the monitors. I might open the security lodge soon.

6:45   Emergency lighting has died. I am using torchlight but don't know how long the batteries will last.

7:00   The torchlight is...oh god it's fading and there is still nothing from outside.

7:15   The banging has started again and not just on the door but all around the walls and...and in my head. I will take some painkillers and hope the noise stops.

7:30   The pain is excruciating now and almost unbearable. I might just be imagining it but I think the banging is getting louder.

7:45   There are people outside. They're screaming and yelling.

I can't tell whether they're inmates or guards.

8.00   I think the doors are about to give. Save me.

No trace of the guards or inmates from Corridors A and B or the Security lodge has ever been found. Police investigations found several pools of strongly congealed blood but little else. All cells and the Security Lodge were empty. In an ongoing search for the presumed escaped criminals, the deaths of Howard and Marie Anne Garcia in the local area of Middleton might be linked, but the police haven't said this in an official document or statement.

Report compiled by:
Kennedy Hepburn-Channing

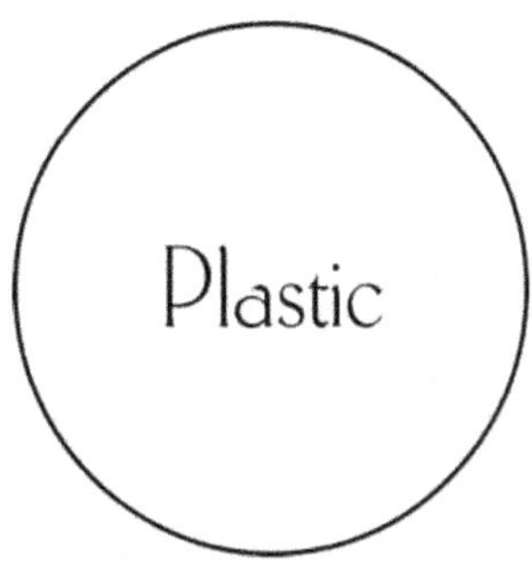

Plastic

David's last patient before he went off shift was a boy called Noah who couldn't stop coughing. Noah's mother, looking harried, apologised before David had a chance to examine the boy.

"I'm sorry, I know that I should have taken him to the doctor rather than bring him here to A&E." She looked nervously at David, whose job title of Head of Department was clearly visible on his badge and whose seniority obviously bothered her, and carried on in a rush. "It's just that our doctor won't see him for another week because he's not urgent, but he's really suffering with it. Can you just please give him something to stop him coughing? It's keeping him awake at night. I mean, look at him, it's making him ill!"

In truth, the boy did look unwell. His skin was the colour of curdled milk and the flesh under his eyes looked bruised with lack of sleep. His breath wheezed and hacked and he shuddered every time he coughed, his thin shoulders twitching like broken birds' wings. David listened to Noah's chest but could find no sign of infection in his lungs. He did not have a temperature.

"What sort of cough is it?" David asked Noah, his stethoscope pressed against the side of the boy's throat. In it, he could hear air whistling raggedly.

"Like I've got something in my mouth that I want to spit out," Noah replied miserably. "I keep coughing and coughing, but it won't come at all. It's just staying there at the back of my tongue."

"Let's have a look then," said David and opened Noah's mouth. "Open as wide as you can." Noah did so, his lips drawing back from his teeth. He inhaled, the sound of it painful and sharp, and he coughed up something green.

Whatever it was came out in a spray of saliva and cocooned in warm coughing, arcing past David's face and performing a graceful glide through the air before hitting the bed with a muffled thump. Noah took a deep, clear breath and said, "That's better!"

David pulled on a pair of disposable gloves and prodded the small mass. It consisted of a clot of green mucus, streaked with darker patches of red. There was something pale at its centre. He felt it carefully and then picked it up. He could not see what the pale shape was, so he ran it under the tap for a moment, washing away the spit and slime. Between his fingers was a small piece of plastic that looked like it had been ripped from a bag, opaque and perhaps a square inch in size. Its edges were ragged and it was thin; there were no markings on either of its sides.

"What have you been chewing on?" David asked Noah, laughing. "You shouldn't eat the bags from the shops, you know. The food they sell is much nicer."

"I didn't!" protested the boy, his face colouring from its previous white to a furious red. "I didn't, Mum, I promise!"

"Hey, it's okay," said David hurriedly, wanting to avoid an argument with either child or mother. "No harm done. Just let me give you a quick check over."

Noah's throat was fine, apart from being a little red and slightly scratched. David advised that he only have soft foods for a day or two, and then watched the two of them leave. Noah's mother was happy with the result; Noah, being scolded for chewing things that he should not, was less happy but would be fine. David smiled to himself, threw the piece of plastic in the waste bin and went home.

David's next shift was two days later and began quietly, but became busier as the hours passed. By its end, he was so tired that he almost missed the conversation between the nurses in the corridor.

"...just spat out a piece of plastic," one nurse was saying. "The mother said he hadn't been chewing anything like that, but he must have been, mustn't he? How can people be so careless?"

"I know, I know," replied the other nurse. "I had one yesterday that had done the same thing. The father said his little girl had been coughing for a couple of days, but that had to be nonsense; the size of the piece she spat out, I can't see it having been there for more than an hour or two without it having choked her. He looked embarrassed when she coughed it up, but he still wouldn't admit anything. It's amazing what parents let their children do, isn't it?"

The nurses walked off down the corridor, leaving David staring after them in surprise. Three incidents in three days? It was odd. Of course, there was a great hospital trade in 'foreign object' stories, but he had never heard of bits of plastic carrier bags being the offending objects before. Idly, he wondered if one of the local shops was using very thin or weak bags, whether it was something that the local council's Health and Safety unit might be interested in, but then his beeper went off and he forgot all about it.

David remembered the plastic a day later, when he got to work to find the staffroom locked and Michael waiting for him. Michael was the hospital's Clinical Director and he did not often come down into the A&E department. David liked him, but their relationship was sometimes a tense one; Michael's constant demands for cost-cutting and target-meeting had adversely impacted on David's team before and David's defence of his department often put him at odds with Michael's strategies.

"Hello, Michael," David said. "We don't often see you down here. Is everything okay?"

"Have you had people coming in and coughing up bits of plastic?" demanded Michael without preamble. He looked nervous.

"One," said David, "but I heard the nurses talking about another couple. Why is the staff room locked?"

"There's been masses this shift. One of your junior doctors, Billings I think his name is, came to see me about it. I'm sure it was just an exercise in covering his back, but you know how it is. I came down here to investigate, just to pacify him really. I thought it might be fun to be back on the floor, you know?" Michael was almost hopping from foot to foot with anxiety by now. "I thought it was just one of those things. I'd check around, sort it out, go back to my office. But then I found... Well, maybe you'd better see it for yourself."

"See what?" demanded David, but Michael had already turned away and was unlocking the staffroom door.

"When I came down, I went around collecting the bits of plastic," said Michael, as though David had not spoken. "At first, I thought that it was just one of those odd coincidences that happen sometimes, like when we get lots of accidents at the same time or outbreaks of disease in different parts of the city all happening at once. I started out by just throwing the bits of plastic away but there were so many of them, I thought I'd better keep some, get them tested. I don't even know what for, really. I just didn't want to miss anything, you know?"

David did know. It was the worst thing imaginable, for a hospital to miss something that was discovered later. It led to lawsuits, investigations, bad publicity. Michael, as Clinical Director, was particularly sensitive to the latter, which he had once described in an unguarded moment as "worse than being punched in the stomach".

"Anyway, I put a load of the plastic in a box in and put it in here. I thought I'd drop it in the lab later, so I went off to talk to the staff. It was quite exciting, really, feeling like I was practising medicine again rather than simply being a manager. I came back to pick the plastic up perhaps an hour after I'd left it, and look." Michael finished unlocking the door and pushed it open. At first, David couldn't see what it was Michael wanted him to look at, but then he saw it.

There was a grey mass covering the coffee table. It looked sickly, like part-cooked dough that had just started to rise. Part of the mass had started to drip over the edge of the table and two long strings of it were hanging down towards the floor. The mass was motionless.

"What is it?" asked David.

"The plastic. It's the plastic. I put it all together in a box and put it on the table and when I came in, there was this mass. I think the plastic's grown."

"Don't be ridiculous," said David, but in his mind he could hear the nurse saying, "*...his little girl had been coughing for a couple of days, but the size of the piece she spat out, I can't see it having been there for more than an hour or two.*" Could it have grown?

David stepped forwards to look at the mass. Behind him, Michael closed the door and locked it again. When David looked at it carefully, he thought he could make out a shape in its middle.

"It's the box," said Michael helplessly. "I saw it as well. I thought someone was playing a joke on me, but then I saw that the box was still in the middle of... whatever this is. It can't be a joke. That's the same box I used for the plastic pieces. Until a few minutes ago, I could recognise it. I wrote on it to make sure no one threw it away and the writing's only just faded away." He gestured helplessly at the grey shape, flapping a hand at it. Taking a deep, uneven breath, he continued.

"And, watch," Michael walked over to the mass and took hold of one of the tendrils. He pulled and the tendril stretched and then snapped. Just like plastic, thought David, and then Michael dropped the long piece on top of the mass.

"Don't watch it. Come over here and look out of the window," said Michael. David did as he was told, confused. "Nothing'll happen if you watch it," carried on Michael.

Through the window, David could see a steady flow of pedestrians and cars into the hospital grounds, a constant stream of humanity needing treatment and answers and reassurance.

"Turn around and look," Michael said.

The torn piece was gone from the top of the mass. Its shape was still there, a curled string, but the edges had merged with the whole as though it had melted. Where Michael had ripped the tendril away, a new one had started to form.

Michael was speaking. "I've rung around," he said. "Every A&E nearby has had people coming in coughing up plastic."

"What's going on?" asked David, feeling as though he were missing something.

"Can't you tell? Can't you guess?"

"No," said David, irritated. He did not like guessing games, and the sight of the mass was disturbing him in ways he could not properly identify or articulate. He wanted Michael to hurry up, to get to the point.

"I think this is the start of a very subtle, very careful invasion. David, we're being invaded."

"Invaded? How? What are you talking about?"

"Think about it: we've always thought that other life would look something like us, that it would act like us, but why should it? Think of the parasites we already know about; some of them act in ways that you'd never be able to guess. What if this is a kind of parasite? And what if invasion isn't like a war, with guns and fights and rockets, but something more insidious?"

"But," said David and then stopped. Thousands and millions of tiny things, he was thinking, none of them harmful by themselves.

We breathe in the spores in the dust, or in water vapour. They take hold, gestate in us, grow from nothing in our throats until they reach a certain size, say about an inch square, and then they...what? Hatch? We spit them out or cough them up and we think *That's small, that's nothing* and we forget it. And some of the pieces die, if they can die, but some meet up and join and grow. Looking closely, he could see that the box at the centre of the mass was nearly gone. The newly-growing tendril was almost at the floor. It had grown without him seeing it move. The older one was already there, and appeared to be weaving itself into the carpet. The fibres around it looked dry and brittle.

"It's taking what it wants from the things it comes into contact with," said Michael. "It's absorbing the box. And do you want to know something else? I don't think it can be killed. Snapping doesn't hurt it, nor cutting. I've tried. I even tried to burn some, in the waste incinerator. It took ages to burn, as if it was muscle rather than plastic. When I turned the incinerator off and left it for a bit, it started to grow again. I could see it through that little observation glass they have in the door; just a lump at the back of the tray, but bigger than it was when I put it in. It's down there now, busily growing and filling the oven. Maybe it's sucking all the strength out of the walls and shelving as it grows. Maybe it'll eventually eat the entire incinerator, burst out and fill the room."

"How can it be growing? That would mean it's alive, and it can't be, can it? It hasn't got a brain or a heart or..." David stopped, confused.

"I don't know. Cells haven't got any of those things either, but they're alive."

"What does it want?"

"I don't know that either. If it's a parasite, it doesn't make sense for it to do more than use us, but I'm not sure it is a true parasite, or at least, not one as we'd understand it. I can't help but think of wasps."

"Wasps?"

"Those ones that paralyse spiders and bury them, then lay their eggs in the hole with them. The eggs hatch, the little babies start life by eating the spider. Maybe that's what it's doing. Using us to incubate its children, so that they're born developed enough to be able to eat. But if that's the case, then what does it eat? I wondered for a while, but I think I've got it now. I thought about the box and it suddenly made sense. Look at the carpet and the table."

David looked and saw with horror that Michael was right. The table legs looked desiccated, had cracked and begun to buckle. The carpet around the tendrils had started to crumble into a colourless dust. It looked as though all the strength and vibrancy had been sucked from it. The mass itself was definitely bigger. The tendrils had started to ease their way across the floor towards the chairs.

"See?" There was a sick kind of exultation in Michael's voice. "Think of all those other dry, lifeless planets around us. Maybe we weren't the only life in the universe, maybe we're just the only life *left*. Besides this, of course," he said, waving tiredly again at the grey mass.

"Just plastic. That's all. Only, it's growing and maybe it'll cover the world soon. I gave this bit a push by putting all the tiny pieces together, gave another piece a push by separating it and putting it somewhere new, downstairs in the incinerator oven, but most of the other bits got flushed away or thrown away or just left in the street. Think of it, all those growing masses in the sewers and the landfills, sucking and stretching and reaching out to each other until they're too big to for us to deal with. I think this is the start of a quiet invasion. All those people coughing, all spitting out bits of plastic? It hasn't stopped yet. How many billions of people are there? And if everyone coughs up a piece, and even if only some of the plastic manages to survive and grow, it's still a lot. And even if we manage to stop it, somehow, how do we know we won't cough more out straight away? When a wasp dies, the spiders aren't safe. There are always more wasps."

"Jesus," David breathed. In his mind, he was seeing the streets he knew, the houses he recognised, covered in a grey sheet like a cocoon. His imagination, unbidden, populated the sheet with dissolving people, their faces twisted in agony and fear as they were sucked into the plastic.

"We have to do something!" he said, gripping hold of Michael's lapels and starting to shake him.

"Do what? Call the police? And tell them what?" Michael pushed David's hands away and stepped back from him, leaning against the sink and looking at the plastic mass. In the time they had been talking, it had grown again.

"Anyway, I've tried. I did do something. I rang a friend of mine in the Department of Health," said Michael, his tone almost conversational. "He didn't laugh at all; no, he connected me through to a very polite man who wouldn't tell me his name but did tell me that the situation was 'under observation'. When I asked what they were doing about it, he said that I'd know soon enough. And then he hung up on me. And I started to think about army units all over the country getting their contamination suits on, about quarantine, about how, if even fire can't destroy this stuff, what they might do to try to beat it.

"I'm going now, David. I only waited to tell you because I always thought we might have been friends, given different circumstances. I'm going to go home and pack some clothes and then I'm going to fill the car with food and drink that'll last. Then I'm going to pick Deborah up from her work and then James up from his school and I'm going to take them somewhere. I know a place miles from the nearest town where we can stay. We might get a month or two, maybe more, before it catches up with us. Maybe less."

"What if you're wrong? What if this is nothing, or if it's easily beaten?"

"Do you think that's likely?" asked Michael. David could not answer, could only watch silently as Michael left the staffroom. Eventually, he wandered back out into the department. Normal chaos was all around, cries and crashes and sobs as life carried on, unaware. He went out into the car park, tilting his head back and looking at the sky. Tears started in his eyes.

All around him, people were coughing.

Also by Simon Kurt Unsworth:

Novels

The Devil's Detective (Del Ray / Doubleday, 2015)

The Devil's Evidence (Del Ray / Doubleday, 2016)

Collections

Lost Places (Ash Tree Press, 2010)

Quiet Houses (Dark Continents Publishing, 2011)

Strange Gateways (PS Publishing, 2014)

Diseases of the Teeth (Black Shuck Books, 2016)

The Martledge Variations (Black Shuck Books, 2018)

Visit Simon Kurt Unsworth at his website:

simonkurtunsworth.wordpress.com

Shadows 18 – The Adventures of Mr Polkington
by Tina Rath

Shadows 19 – Green Fingers
by Dan Coxon

Shadows 20 – Three Mothers, One Father
by Sean Hogan

Shadows 21 – Uneasy Beginnings
by Simon Kurt Unsworth &
Benjamin Kurt Unsworth

blackshuckbooks.co.uk/shadows